REBIRDS

MASTER MIMICS

KATIE
LAJINESS

AWESOME ANIMAL
POWERS

Big Buddy Books

An Imprint of Abdo Publishing
abdopublishing.com

abdopublishing.com

Published by Abdo Publishing, a division of ABDO, PO Box 398166, Minneapolis, Minnesota 55439.
Copyright © 2019 by Abdo Consulting Group, Inc. International copyrights reserved in all countries.
No part of this book may be reproduced in any form without written permission from the publisher.
Big Buddy Books™ is a trademark and logo of Abdo Publishing.

Printed in the United States of America, North Mankato, Minnesota.
052018
092018

THIS BOOK CONTAINS
RECYCLED MATERIALS

Cover Photo: Arco Images GmbH/Alamy Stock Photo.
Interior Photos: Andreas Ruhz/Shutterstock (p. 23); Arco Images GmbH/Alamy Stock Photo (p. 30);
    Auscape International Pty Ptd/Alamy Stock Photo (p. 25); CraigRJD/Getty Images (pp. 5, 9,
    21, 27, 29); dannogan/Getty Images (p. 17); Jiri Herout/Shutterstock (p. 11); Mastamak/Getty
    Images (p. 7); McPhoto/Volz/Alamy Stock Photo (p. 15); Roger Powell/NiS/Minden Pictures/
    Getty Images (p. 19).

Coordinating Series Editor: Tamara L. Britton
Contributing Editor: Jill Roesler
Graphic Design: Jenny Christensen, Erika Weldon

Library of Congress Control Number: 2017961384

Publisher's Cataloging-in-Publication Data

Names: Lajiness, Katie, author.
Title: Lyrebirds: Master mimics / by Katie Lajiness.
Other titles: Master mimics
Description: Minneapolis, Minnesota : Abdo Publishing, 2019. | Series: Awesome animal
    powers | Includes online resources and index.
Identifiers: ISBN 9781532115011 (lib.bdg.) | ISBN 9781532155734 (ebook)
Subjects: LCSH: Lyrebirds--Juvenile literature. | Birdsongs--Juvenile literature. | Birds--
    Vocalization--Juvenile literature. | Animals--Australia--Juvenile literature.
Classification: DDC 598.822--dc23

CONTENTS

THE LYREBIRD

The world is full of awesome, powerful animals. Lyrebirds (leye-UHR-buhrds) live in Australia. Many know them as master **mimics**. These birds can change their birdcall to sound like 20 different bird **species**.

The superb lyrebird is well known in Australia. It is even on the country's ten-cent coin.

BOLD BODIES

Lyrebirds are one of the world's largest songbirds. The superb lyrebird weighs about two pounds (1 kg). The Albert's lyrebird weighs slightly less.

Both kinds have dark brown top feathers. The feathers around their bellies are a lighter color. They have reddish-brown markings on their chests and throats. Their feet, legs, and beaks are black.

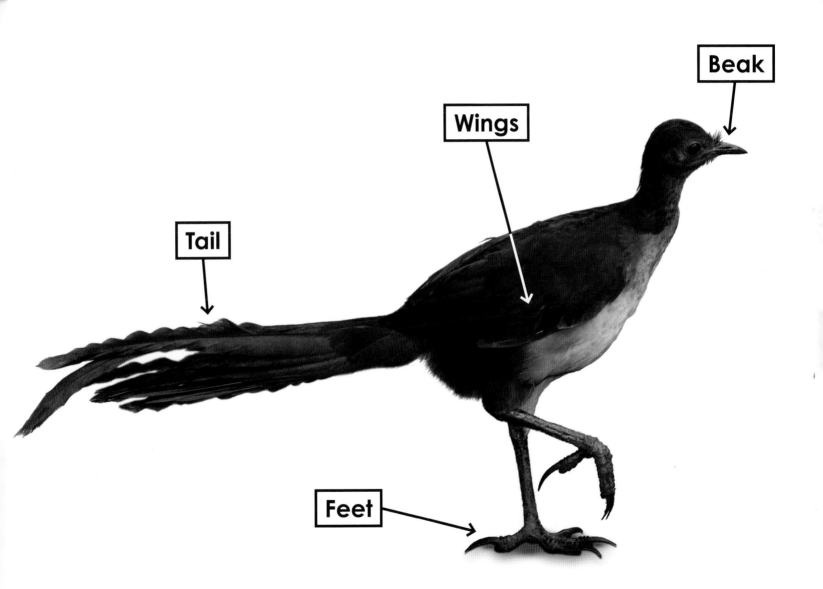

THAT'S AWESOME!

Lyrebirds can **mimic** birdcalls and human sounds. These sounds include car alarms, chain saws, and even camera **shutters**. Others can sound like whistles, car engines, or crying babies.

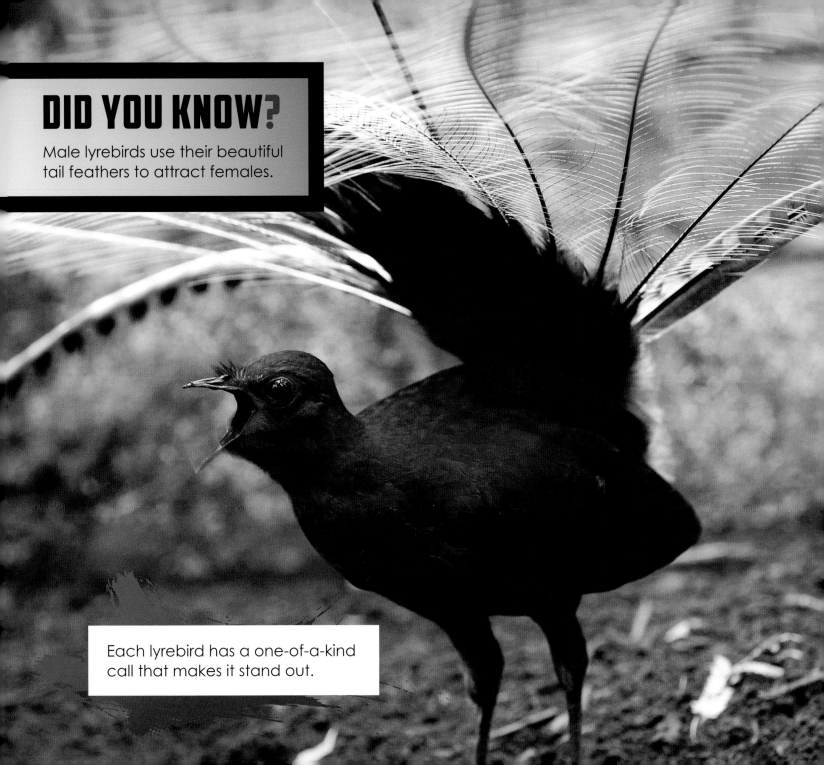

DID YOU KNOW?

Male lyrebirds use their beautiful tail feathers to attract females.

Each lyrebird has a one-of-a-kind call that makes it stand out.

During **breeding** season, male lyrebirds sing and dance to attract females. Their uncommon vocal organs allow them to **mimic** other birds' **mating** calls.

From May to August, lyrebirds sing up to four hours a day. One song can last up to 20 minutes!

The Albert's lyrebird was named after Prince Albert of England. He was Queen Victoria's husband.

Superb lyrebirds live in the **rain forests** of southeastern Australia. And they also live in Tasmania.

Albert's lyrebirds live only in southeastern Australia. They live in rain forests, **gullies**, and along mountain ridges.

WORLD?

■ = **WHERE LYREBIRDS LIVE**

ARCTIC OCEAN

North America

Europe

Asia

PACIFIC OCEAN

NORTH ATLANTIC OCEAN

PACIFIC OCEAN

South America

Africa

INDIAN OCEAN

Australia

SOUTH ATLANTIC OCEAN

N
W   E
S

Tasmania

DAILY LIFE

Lyrebirds spend much of their day looking for food. During **breeding** season, males focus on finding a **mate**.

These birds are shy around humans and other animals. But they make themselves noticeable by having the world's loudest birdcall.

Females can mate when they are about six years old. Males become fully mature when they are eight years old.

Lyrebirds' uncommon **vocal cords** make them great singers. But they also have an excellent sense of smell. Lyrebirds can smell food that may be hidden on the forest floor. They can also smell if there is anything poisonous in the area.

In 1931, the lyrebird's mating call was recorded. The 11-minute audio clip was then played on the radio in Australia.

A LYREBIRD'S LIFE

During **breeding** season, a male superb lyrebird builds several dirt mounds. He uses them like a stage to show off for the females. On the mound, the male bird spreads his beautiful tail over his head. Then he sings songs to draw a **mate's** attention.

DID YOU KNOW?

The lyrebird got its name from an instrument called a lyre. The male's tail feathers look similar to the curved arms of a lyre.

Male lyrebirds do not grow colorful tails until they are about four years old.

Lyrebirds can fly, but they do not often do so. Their short, round wings do not allow for long flights. Instead, their wings help them glide short distances and hop from tree to tree.

These birds use their strong legs to run on the ground. This is also how they get away from **predators**.

At night, lyrebirds sleep on low branches or on the ground. That way, they can stay close to their ground nests.

FAVORITE FOODS

Lyrebirds use their large feet to find food. Their long claws help dig through leaves and soil.

Then, the lyrebirds' sharp, curved beaks pick insects out of the dirt. Lyrebirds also enjoy eating worms, lizards, frogs, and some seeds.

Lyrebirds mostly eat alone. But mother birds bring food back to the nest for their babies.

BIRTH

Every season, male birds **mate** with many females. **Pregnant** females build dome-shaped nests on the forest floor. They use nearby sticks, ferns, feathers, moss, and roots.

In her nest, a female lays only one brown, blotchy egg. She sits on the egg for six weeks until it hatches.

After it hatches, a young lyrebird stays in the nest for six to ten weeks.

DEVELOPMENT

A young lyrebird is called a chick. A chick is born with white feathers. But soon, the feathers turn reddish-brown.

After **breeding**, the mother lyrebird stays close to the nest. The chick is still too young to defend itself if a **predator** enters the nest. If a stranger does enter the nest, the chick shrieks loudly for its mother.

A lyrebird can live up to 30 years in the wild.

FUTURE

The lyrebird has a healthy **population**. But every day, humans cut down trees in the **rain forest**. This is destroying many lyrebird homes. Because of that, some people fear that the lyrebird population will go down.

Luckily, environment groups fight to save the rain forests. If the rain forests can stay safe, so can lyrebirds.

The superb lyrebird was first discovered in 1788.

FAST FACTS

ANIMAL TYPE: Bird

SIZE: About 31 to 41 inches (80 to 103 cm)

WEIGHT: Two pounds (1 kg) or less

HABITAT: Rain forests, gullies, and mountain ridges

DIET: Insects, lizards, frogs, and worms

AWESOME ANIMAL POWER: Their ability to mimic up to 20 different birdcalls, as well as human sounds.

GLOSSARY

breed to produce animals by mating.

gully a trench worn in the earth by running water.

mate to join as a couple in order to reproduce, or have babies. A mate is a partner to join with in order to reproduce.

mimic to copy what you see or hear.

population a group of people or animals living in a certain place.

predator a person or animal that hunts and kills animals for food.

pregnant having one or more babies growing within the body.

rain forest a woodland with a high annual rainfall and very tall trees and that is often found in tropical regions.

shutter a device in a camera that opens to let in light when a picture is taken.

species (SPEE-sheez) living things that are very much alike.

vocal cords the muscles involved in producing the voice.

ONLINE RESOURCES | **Booklinks** NONFICTION NETWORK FREE! ONLINE NONFICTION RESOURCES

To learn more about lyrebirds, visit **abdobooklinks.com**. These links are routinely monitored and updated to provide the most current information available.

INDEX